# A VOYAGE in the CLOUDS

### The (Mostly) True Story of the First International Flight by Balloon in 1785

Matthew Olshan

Illustrated by Sophie Blackall

MARGARET FERGUSON BOOKS • Farrar Straus Giroux • New York

"Our big day at last!" cried Dr. Jeffries, leaping from bed. He flung open the shutters and lifted his dog, Henry, to the window. "Isn't the view across the English Channel splendid? See that smudge on the horizon? It's France. The sky is fair. The air is frosty. The wind is undecided. It looks like a fine day to fly from England to France!"

What do you say, old chum?

It was *January 7, 1785*.
In the year and a half since the flight
of the first manned balloon,
it seemed that everyone was flying.
An Italian had flown.
A Scot had flown.
A woman had flown.
Even a sheep had flown.

But no one had flown
from one country to another.
Dr. Jeffries and his pilot,
Monsieur Blanchard,
wanted to be the first.

Jeffries dressed and went to find Blanchard. He tapped on the Frenchman's door.

Wakey-wakey!

When there was no answer, he opened it.

Rise and shine, you slugabed.

But Blanchard wasn't in his room.

Jeffries found Blanchard at the parade ground. He was entertaining a large crowd with a violin while his dog, Henri, snoozed at his feet. A military band was playing along. Pretty girls were tossing him flowers. The balloon was full and straining at its ropes.

Why didn't you wait for me, Blanchard?

Look who's here, Henri. Shall we tell Dr. Jeffries the bad news?

Bad news? What bad news?

With all our provisions, the balloon cannot carry the weight of two men and two dogs. Only one man. Me. And only one dog. Henri.

Jeffries had taken careful notes the
night before. He decided to unload
the balloon and put each item back on
the scale to see if anything had changed.

"Let's see . . ." he said. "Three sacks
of sand: thirty-three pounds.
*Check.*
Aerial car and anchor: seventy pounds.
*Check.*
A violin and a bow,
one travel thermometer,
one umbrella,
two cork jackets,
a bottle of brandy,
and one roast chicken.
So far so good.
All right, Henry. Here, boy!
Hop on the scale. Good.
Your turn, Henri.
Now me.
*Check, check, check.*
Monsieur Blanchard,
please get on the scale."

"Really, Doctor,"
Blanchard said, blushing.
"This is too much."

"Up you go," Jeffries said.

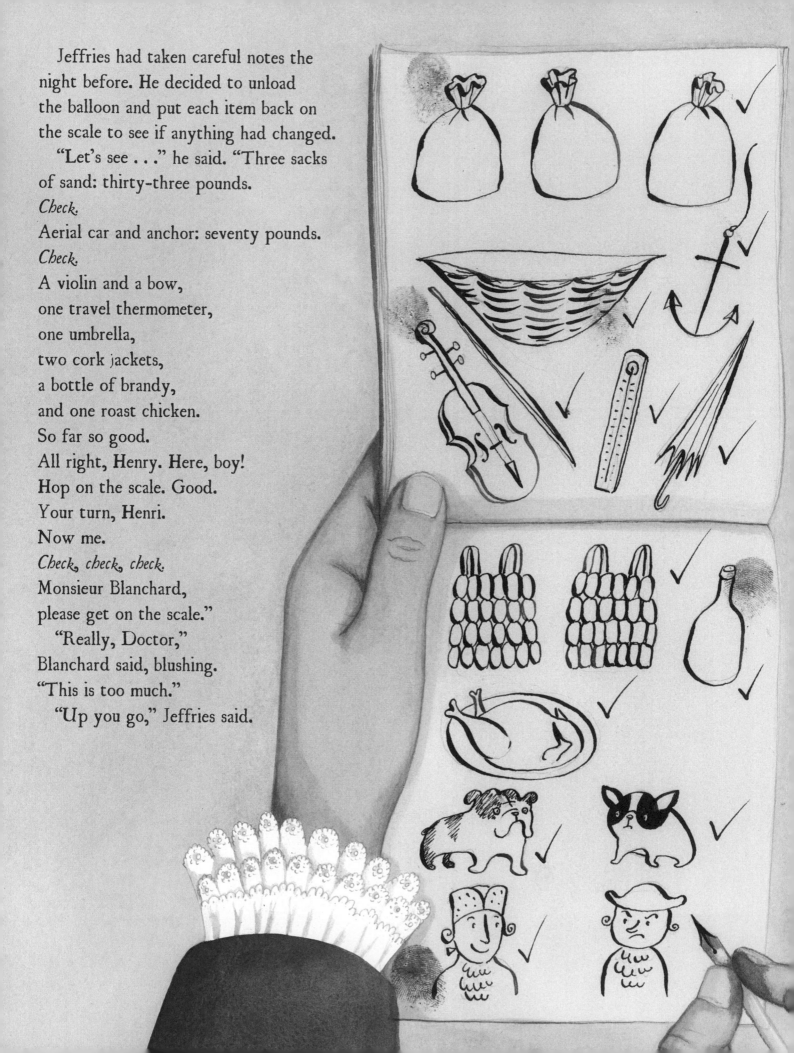

Blanchard reattached the aerial car to the balloon, and Jeffries loaded the provisions.

Soon it was time to lift off.

"Three cheers for Dr. Jeffries!" shouted a soldier, who handed him the Union Jack.

"Oh, no," Jeffries said with a wave of his fur-lined glove. "Three cheers for England!"

Then a girl in a pink bonnet tossed Blanchard a French flag.

"And five more cheers for France!" Blanchard said.

Jeffries wanted to make a speech, but before he could say one word Blanchard cut the tethers, and the balloon leaped into the air.

The winds aloft were brisk. The balloon overtook a warship, which fired its cannon in salute.

The balloon rose ever higher. The wind
picked up, and the aerial car began to sway back and
forth. Down below, there was nothing but gray water.

"There, there, old fellow," Jeffries said, patting Henry.
"Not to worry."

The swaying didn't seem to bother Blanchard. "All
of this rowing has made me hungry," he said.

"What do you say, Doctor? Care for a snack?"

"Maybe later," Jeffries said.
Blanchard tied a napkin around his
neck and tucked into the roast chicken.
"Good," he said. "More for me."
After his meal, the Frenchman had a
little nap.

Up they floated into the clouds.

As the air got thinner,
the balloon got bigger.

It swelled and swelled.
Soon, it looked ready to pop.

But the Frenchman was
snoring soundly.

Next went the violin and the bow, the travel thermometer, and the umbrella.

"More, more!" shouted Blanchard.

Over went the oars, rudder, and anchor.

"We're headed into the water!" cried Jeffries.

"What's left?" Blanchard said.

"The decorations," Jeffries said.

Out went the basket's silk lining and all the gold tassels.

They hesitated to throw the flags.

The flags took flight like colorful birds.

"There's nothing left to throw!" Jeffries said.
"Except our clothes," Blanchard said.
Over the side went shirts, shoes, jackets, and
trousers—everything but their underwear.

"Time to put on our cork jackets," said Blanchard.
"Oops," said Jeffries. "I seem to have thrown mine overboard."
"Then I'll throw mine away, too."

Jeffries looked at Blanchard.
Blanchard looked at Jeffries.

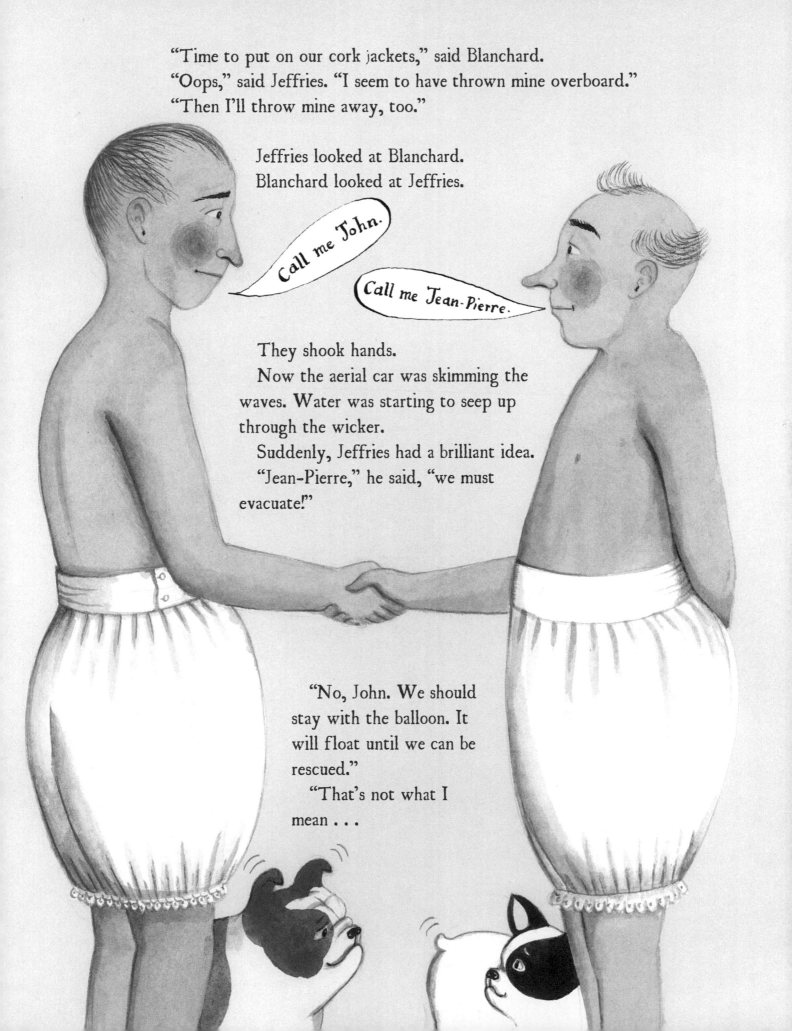

Call me John.

Call me Jean-Pierre.

They shook hands.
Now the aerial car was skimming the
waves. Water was starting to seep up
through the wicker.
Suddenly, Jeffries had a brilliant idea.
"Jean-Pierre," he said, "we must
evacuate!"

"No, John. We should
stay with the balloon. It
will float until we can be
rescued."
"That's not what I
mean . . .

"When was the last time you had a pee?"
Blanchard shrugged. "I suppose every little
bit helps."

You're next, Henry.

Inch by inch, the balloon climbed above the waves.

"We ascend, John!" said Blanchard.

"We're saved, Jean-Pierre!" said Jeffries.

Up, up it went until they were once again high above the water.

"It's quite cold, no?" said Blanchard.

"I could use a fur coat right about now," said Jeffries.

Their teeth were chattering as they passed over the French shore.

"John, your lips are blue," Blanchard said.

"Yours, too, Jean-Pierre. But look! We've crossed La Manche," said Jeffries.

"Which is to say, the English Channel," said Blanchard.

Never had land looked so beautiful. A great crowd was there to welcome them.

"Look, Henry! We made it to France," said Jeffries.

"We're home, Henri!" said Blanchard.

But the two dogs were curled up together, sleeping soundly.

The aerial car bounced from treetop to treetop.

Finally, Jeffries managed to wrap his arms around a branch while Blanchard emptied the rest of the gas from the balloon.

Everyone cheered when the aerial car touched down. Jeffries and Blanchard had made the first international flight. They were heroes!

# AUTHOR'S NOTE

DR. JOHN JEFFRIES
(1745–1819)

JEAN-PIERRE BLANCHARD
(1753–1809)

On January 7, 1785, Dr. John Jeffries and Jean-Pierre Blanchard set out to make the world's first international flight by crossing the English Channel in a balloon. They had flown together once before—an uneventful short flight from London to the nearby countryside.

Dr. Jeffries was born in Boston but considered himself an Englishman. He volunteered to serve in the Royal Navy during the Revolutionary War. After the war, he lived in exile in England until 1789, when he returned to the United States. He had little experience with ballooning, but he put up the money for the expeditions.

Jean-Pierre Blanchard, on the other hand, had been aloft many times. He was responsible for supplying the balloon and the hydrogen gas to fill it. Blanchard was interested in finding new ways to steer a balloon. He devised a set of wings that he rowed like oars. His "aerial car" also had a rudder, just like a boat. In 1785, everybody thought the atmosphere was a liquid!

Unfortunately, the two men did not get along. Blanchard didn't think Jeffries was man enough to make the flight. Jeffries thought Blanchard was a show-off and a trickster.

*A Voyage in the Clouds* is based on their perilous—and successful—cross-Channel flight, which took two hours and forty-seven minutes. Most of the story is factual, as recounted in Jeffries's monograph, *A Narrative of the Two Aerial Voyages of Doctor Jeffries with Mons. Blanchard,* which was presented to the Royal Society in 1785. Blanchard did try to fool Jeffries with a lead-lined vest in the days leading up to the flight, and the two men did, in fact, pee over the side to lighten the balloon when it looked as though they were headed for a crash landing. You can find the original monograph at archive.org/stream/narrativeoftwoae00jeff.

However, I did take a few liberties with the story. For instance, there's no record that Blanchard napped during the flight, or that their plunge from the sky was the result of carelessness.

As for the dogs, Blanchard was known for taking a lapdog on his balloon rides, and Jeffries had taken his own little dog on their first flight together, but there's no mention of a dog on board the day they crossed the Channel.

Even so, I like to think there might have been.

Fill me up
—M.O.

For *Marnie and Jerry and Ben*
—S.B.

Farrar Straus Giroux Books for Young Readers
175 Fifth Avenue, New York 10010

Text copyright © 2016 by Matthew Olshan
Pictures copyright © 2016 by Sophie Blackall
All rights reserved
Printed in China by RR Donnelley Asia
Printing Solutions Ltd.,
Dongguan City, Guangdong Province
Designed by Sophie Blackall
and Roberta Pressel
First edition, 2016

1 3 5 7 9 10 8 6 4 2

mackids.com

Library of Congress
Cataloging-in-Publication Data

Names: Olshan, Matthew, author. | Blackall, Sophie, illustrator.
Title: A voyage in the clouds : the (mostly) true story of the
   first international flight by balloon in 1785 / Matthew Olshan ;
   pictures by Sophie Blackall.
Description: First edition. | New York : Margaret Ferguson Books /
   Farrar Straus Giroux, 2016. | Summary: "A picture book inspired
   by the true story of how the first international flight was an
   Englishman and a Frenchman who rode in a balloon across the
   English Channel"— Provided by publisher.
Identifiers: LCCN 2015036614 | ISBN 9780374329549 (hardback)
Subjects: LCSH: Jeffries, John, 1745–1819—Juvenile fiction. | Blanchard,
   Jean-Pierre, 1753–1809—Juvenile fiction. | CYAC: Jeffries, John,
   1745–1819—Fiction. | Blanchard, Jean-Pierre, 1753–1809—Fiction. |
   Balloon ascensions—Fiction. | BISAC: JUVENILE FICTION /
   Transportation / Aviation. | JUVENILE FICTION / Historical /
   Exploration & Discovery. | JUVENILE NONFICTION /
   Biography & Autobiography / Historical.
Classification: LCC PZ7.O51788 Vo 2016 | DDC [E]—dc23
LC record available at https://lccn.loc.gov/2015036614

Our books may be purchased in bulk for promotional,
educational, or business use. Please contact your local
bookseller or the Macmillan Corporate and Premium
Sales Department at (800) 221-7945 ext. 5442
or by e-mail at MacmillanSpecialMarkets
@macmillan.com.